Pour Maman et Juliette

C.L.

ISBN: 1-903078-55-5

ISBN: 1-903078-56-3 PB

First published in the United Kingdom in 2001 by Siphano Picture Books Ltd.

Regent's Place, 338 Euston Road, London NW1 3BT

www.siphano.com

British Library Cataloguing-in-Publication Data

A catalogue record for this book is available from the British Library

Colour separation: Vivliosynergatiki, Athens, Greece

Printed in Italy by Grafiche AZ, Verona

CHARLOTTE LABARONNE

Just One Roar!

SIPHANO PICTURE BOOKS · LONDON

Matthew didn't like playing
with the other children at school.

"I'm a tough alligator,"
he would say. "I don't want
to play with sissies."

When the teacher read stories, Matthew made a loud noise, just to annoy everybody. He walked around with the bass drum –

BOOM BOOM BOOM!

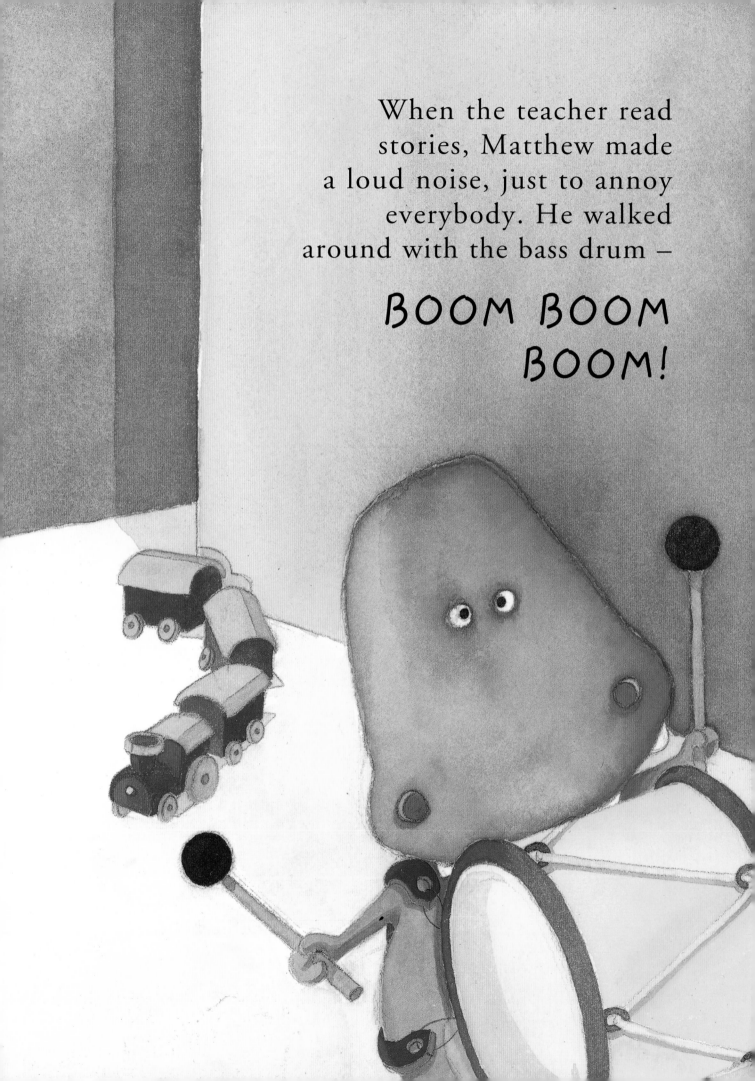

At drawing-time,
they heard that a lion
called Alex was coming
to join the class.

"A lion – tough
and strong like me!"
thought Matthew.
"I know we're going
to be friends."

Matthew was
eager to meet Alex.
He waited for a long
time at the school gate...

...but when Alex finally
appeared, Matthew couldn't believe it –
Alex was a girl!

The other children all introduced
themselves to Alex and invited her to play.

But not Matthew.
Matthew was cross
that Alex was a girl,
and he decided
to make her life

MISERABLE!

When Alex walked by, Matthew
spilled juice on her teddy-bear.

He was going to run over
the teddy-bear as well, but
in the end he didn't,
because Alex wasn't
watching.

"I'll make her notice," said Matthew.

When he saw Alex building a block tower, he walked past, giving it a kick. It came down with a

CRASH!

Then he got out his tuba and blasted it
in her ear.

When she went to do some
painting, Matthew
found a tin
of red finger paint,
crept up behind
her easel...

... and splashed
red splotches all over it.

That did it.

Alex opened her mouth
and let out one enormous...
terrifying...

ROOOOARRF

Matthew jumped back
in alarm. He had never
heard anybody make
a noise like that
before!

RR!

The other children
were very impressed
with Alex's roar.
"You even scared Matthew!"
they said to her.

At playtime, they all
went out into the yard.
But Matthew was
so embarrassed, he stayed
inside and read a book.

After a while Alex came inside too,
and sat down near Matthew. She looked
to see what he was reading.

When she got up, Matthew
looked to see where she was going...

...and when he saw her sitting
by herself on the see-saw, he asked
nicely if he could sit on the other end.

After they had see-sawed
for a while, they decided
to go on the tyre swing.

Some other children
came to play on it too.

Then they went
on the climbing bars.
    "Let's all
make a noise!"
said Matthew,
and everybody
shouted, to see
who could shout
the loudest.
Alex shouted too!

When story-time came,
they sat down
around the teacher.
She was surprised because
everybody was sitting
so quietly – even Matthew!

And this time, Matthew
didn't play the bass drum –
he sat next to Alex instead.
They were going
to play an even better
Make-a-Noise game
in the yard tomorrow!